SHOULD THIS SEE THE LIGHT OF DAY?

Publisher's Note: We do not approve of page numbers. A book starts and closes whenever it feels like.

SHOULD THIS SEE THE LIGHT OF DAY?

by Zak Ferguson

PART I:

COMPACT

Do I?/Shall I?

Do I start at the beginning? Shall I start in the middle? Shall I start at the end that you have super glued together from various fragments of maps from all over the world? Shall I follow your lead? Shall I translate dog barks as subliminal tracking dots part of the cat's meow-app? Do I unwrap the Christmas gifts that my neighbours have piled up into a glorious pyramid, oppressing my sense of societal bliss? Do I share with you the shall I segments of my brain, delivered on the post-mortem giggler's favourite metal tray? Shall I ask for a CAT scan? Shall I ask them for a cat whilst waiting for said CAT scan? Do I start cooking the turkey an hour earlier than is necessary? Shall I ponder the as ever ponderable which is, can an experimental piece be captured, when it is reliant on fonts, their sizes and typography, when spoken aloud? Shall I ask for more vinegar on my chips, even though I am half hours walk away from the Fish and Chip parlour, and have eaten most of them? Shall I proffer the empty newspaper wrapping and state, "Not enough vinegar, can I have some?" Shall I be surprised if they look at me as if I had dragged their 98 year old mother, or grandmother in by the remainder of her hair, butt naked, covered in satanic symbols I had gleaned from the picture books these old fuckers love to covet and obsess over, all whilst she has a soppy grin on her face, that screams, *"A man has never shown me such passion in decades!"* Do I respond with, "I only realised after I had consumed the package. Now, I feel kind of, I don't know, out of myself, because the vinegar didn't hit right, you know?" Shall I accept the vinegar being shaken, wank-handedly, into the proffered, and saturated in grease, and yes, vinegar, newspaper wrapping these Fish and Chip sellers cannot quite get away from using(?) Shall I do the same thing when I have eaten my Take Away Burger, call them hours down the line and ask if they could provide a reverse enema, to pump curry sauce up into my stomach, and to coat my intestines with that most delicious and specifically British sauce? Shall I buy a copy of the 20th anniversary edition of some JK Rowling harry Putter-Potter book, to later find weird acronyms that hint that JK Rowling was always a shyster from the start? Shall I buy a copy of the 20th anniversary edition of some JK Rowling harry Puttering-Putter-Potter book, to later find out that this whole warped notion of her being anti-this, anti-that, is par for the course, nowadays, for any writer with more than a grand in their bank account? Shall I recommend some books for you to read; here is a list of them, TRANSPARENT by Nicola Barker, REVERSED FORECAST by Nicola Barker, BEHINDLINGS by Nicola Barker, WIDE OPEN by Nicola Barker, H (A) P P Y by Nicola Barker, everything by Nicola Barker; except for DARKMANS as after 400 pages I had to use it as a weapon, it produced such energy in me. Do I state the obvious, that this is not autofiction, auto-auto-auto-alternatives to expressing oneself. Shall I watch Gogglebox on my own, a weird reality TV show about people watching telly, whilst we are watching them watch telly, opining on their tastes and personalities all based upon to how they respond to watching telly, and judging them on how they watch telly. Do I admit this is paradoxical or shall I just let it simmer, like the brandy in the family favourite saucepan? Shall I ask my partner to give me a massage knowing that she has a fucked up back and suffers far worse than I can ever imagine? Do I travel to the ends of the earth to attain a stile embedded with sharp, lethal, unextractable diamonds? Do I ask the Roman's haunting my every waking moment the most important of questions; Nascio, how do you represent birth? Nascio are you always bloated with a food baby, representing pregnancy? Nascio are you a God dressed as a Goddess, all so you can eat all you want and not get criticised? Naenia, do you lament the funerals that you are meant to funerarily lament over and for? Funerarily, that is a word, now, why? Shall I tell you why? It is because once a word has been conquered by the mouth, projected amongst the masses, passed from one to the other, cropping up in conversations, important conversations where your control and unlimited power over language is up for discussion, introducing itself like a nude model from an oversized cake, declaring, "coooeeeeeee, here I am, passed from the mouth of somebody who should and does know better," - that then implements the word, makes it real, makes it true, makes it what it is, a word in existence; and thus, it is as it is! Shall I continue asking the Gods on their interpretation of Heliogabalus, and how committed they believed he was to the incestuous permutations his ilk carried like heavy pumice-stones around their necks? Shall I tell you, their response? Do I? Shall I? Shall I tell you that Neptune much preferred being known for earthquakes and good grapevine curling, then being assigned as God of the seas? Do I tell you that Caelestis took on the virginal aspects merely because she perfected self-pleasure, and no one could know that she bean-flicked herself into oblivion most nights, her

sweat adding salt to Neptune's waters; living
life as the virginal deity built out of various
other deities, the one's that came forward in the
near future, or in the moment of her
presentation; she didn't fuck, she didn't birth,
she merely self-pleasured, shall this be
admitted? It has been.

Incantations/Verbal Frustrations

Incantations come in various genres. I am being serious. They do. If they are weaved into science fiction, it is entitled, *futurist optimism*/or *futurist pessimism*, dependent upon the character speaking/thinking. If it is an incantation in horror, it is supernal, paranormal, supernatural, it is *evil*. If it is just a personal incantation for motivation, for control, for focus, for the steadying of mind and limbs, it is a *personal journey of mental healing*/or a *faux mental execution of control*, created by obsessive determination. Incantatory words producing mouth flapping flaps. Not cheeks. Mouth flaps, part jowl, part sagging excess skin around one's goitre, converging to create what looks like compressed toad-like cheeks. The words gather, the unspoken, yet un-enunciated relics of the mouth-sphere, coated in stem cells wailing like newborn babies to be extracted by Doctor Paolo Macchiarini in some false video documentation, pertaining to the legality of his illegal experiments – rippled in mycelium that embodies the history that we share genetically with our great-great-great-great-grand-greatly-grand-great grandfather. No holla or bellow. It is the impact of the unreleased.

Pucker up, mate! Incantations that produced bagpipe animal pelt alterations to your human pelt, the unreleased forcing breath as a gale force wind, that produce hilariously ugly facial distortions that are forcing your ears upward, downward, wiggling them in the way Mr. Bean can do. Mr. Bean, not Mr. Ben, Mr. Bean, played by Rowan Atkinson. *Oh teddy, Bean,* yes, *Bean*! Say it in that dunce-y Mr. Bean way. We have all done it. Looking in the mirror, perfecting our ugliest of faces. Why him? Why Rowan and not me? Well, it is all luck, *kid*! Say kid in the Harrison Ford voice we all silently perform in our minds every time that grumpy grandad's image appears on our digital devices. *Kid! Hey, kid!* Incantatory mouth blowing, forcing your nostrils to widen like blackholes that can transport you anywhere at any time, apart from taking you to the destination you most want to go back to, which is your bed. Cheek's inflating, ears lodging themselves into random positions, settling down for the next decade or two – it takes a lot out of an ear to travel from their original positions to the top of your head, to the side of your neck, nestling beneath your chinny-chin-chins. Ears moving from their predestined places of existence, by muscle movement and facial constraints being tugged, altered to such dense degrees that the reality of a face and all its potentialities take on a Jim Carrey cadence and form. Where were you when the ears decided to crawl up onto the back of your head, the left one canting at an angle, being a little bit bigger than the rest, using its deformity in a further deformity, to make an example of itself, rightfully, and wrongfully, so you looked like some deformed creature/flesh art piece from David Cornenberg's underwhelming *Crimes of the Future* – all for the world and its loathsome lot to laugh, take photos and post on social media. Come on, *kid*! Get ahead of them, take a photo, make up some sob story, create a whole identity around your bagpipe playing ear catastrophe. Get all leading surgeons and big networks to pay you big money for your story, and the latter stories that will be built from the initial NBC story, all because you sat down with one or two "experimental" surgeons who were nothing but con artists wanting to use your ear adventures as excuse to butcher a human body; confused as to what the message of Eli Roth's Hostel films were. Ears in awkward positions to never again be put back in their rightful, clear and human compatible positions/places. Mouth gestures formulating the freed pigeon that had its ankle broken and reset and broken again because this pigeon tamer and racer had no clue what it took to rear pigeons and guide them across the various skylines of our planet called

DIRT. Popping on VHS tapes of old, the colour, the striations, the aesthetical distortions so specific, wonderous, nostalgic, uniquely singular, and universal all at the same bloody time, and though no older than a few decades, it has taken on antiquated proportions. Emblems. Emblematic. Totemic. Icons in a digital age. VHS was not digital, it was analog, and analog was scripture. You took out your old brown-faux-leatherbound cassette tapes all so you could try and capture the modern in the old; applying a dated system that is much missed, and replicated by advanced filmmaking apps, to give it a glitch, a grain, a visual stutter. for you to tape over, only for the recording you attempted to tap over not work, but further corrupt the VHS materials and the subject materials weaved, immortalised, now made defunct because you wanted to try and record the Netflix App opener, heralding with its unique **der-dum!** Flipping through catalogue books, hoping that the glossy pages do not come apart and tear, and dissolve with your favourite kind of glue, a Pritt stick. You want more for yourself and your family. Your family consisting of one hundred collages, on cheap cardboard, no thicker than your local tax collectors' letters, and you try to attain the more especially for your children – your collages, by building and promoting for free, whether successfully or unsuccessfully it doesn't matter on Instagram. You want for much, and do not want for much, unless the local ASDA (WAL-MART in the US of A) doesn't stock your favourite crisps (potato chips for those in the US of A) – you scream in that aisle, the aisle that used to be aisle 18, but then was shifted to aisle 20, that then went back to being aisle 18, but it isn't aisle 18 but aisle 17 1/2 as they have changed things, shelving units around so much that they do not number aisles, they name them – aisle this, that, aisle that and this, because people are stupid and need an overlarge sign stating EGGS and ALL RELATED EGG BASED PRODUCTS for you to still go, what aisle is it on? Derp! You pile them up, the collages, not the eggs, but if you are into eggs, how imperfect they are juxtaposed to the more higher grade type of egg, you capture them with polaroid, and then scan said polaroid, only to merely alter it to resemble a photo that could and could not be captured by the daguerreotype camera, for your collage art is always dictated by collage gods; and what is a god if not a sneaky, crafty, lying, deceitful, catastrophising intrusive "being". You give up. You lose out. You cook your meal on a low heat, extremely limited by your lack of kitchen utensils, and believing a low heat over hours will be cheaper than a high heat and have the meal all done within half an hours' time. You speak aloud, hoping that the words you slave over come to life, in the same way such images are conjured from your minds when reading. If you are monotone, some fill in the gaps, the so-called blanks, and have a better understanding of your verse than you ever will. You speak aloud, hoping that the words you type, that you write in long hand can come alive, and you force it by verbal pitches, by gestures, and a performance, that will be translated differently for each person watching/listening/or make-believe braille touching as you do your thing; the same goes for reading, not always, but most often, the words are so precise, so clear, so well formatted and written, that the visual becomes a shared universal iconographic twin, multiplied by the billions; that you finally snap your fingers, Bingo!/Eureka! – coming out of your clouded whimsy and self-centredness, and grasp that is why fanboys and fangirls get so touchy about film adaptations. You scream so the piece is delivered into bones and all. You screech because you need it to be felt as much as heard. You do silly voices all because you feel, in that moment of performance, it will lend something, not just to the words, but to yourself personally/your identity as an artist. You shift. You hit delete. You dribble prose like you dribbled marmite and paracetamol combos that your mother stupidly thought would help the medicine go down. Incantatory means to reprogramme. It means to illicit motion, sensations lost when sitting on a hardbacked chair that somehow, he battled on through in our education between the years year 3 to 11. Remember the years where we all had to sit cross legged and look up to our teacher, forced to look upon them, and them down onto us. What a weird psychological thing to execute in the physical for such young bucks and buckerellas. I am at your feet, Miss, not Mr. I am bearing witness to your throne. Metal legs. Metal frame. Frayed weaving, with that pasty tallow stuffing coming out, that some kids, on the sly picked, and later got caught doing, and were punished by... losing out on golden time. Sharing these phrases. Sharing these words. Sharing these observations, these events, what makes them so special? Is it the voice I am hoping to achieve in perfecting when it comes to reading them aloud to an audience of one, or none? My grasp on the English language has always been fragile. Feeble Ferguson, spitting, frothing, mispronouncing words. You encompass all that has been criticised, your aggression, your weirdness, and have weaponised it, into a clownish, buffoonish personality; because that one time that you mispronounced it, a word, any old word, and how you irrationally, without thought or composition, worded it bizarrely, you, you felt it was now your right to continue saying the word as you had initially, in that stupid moment said it, aloud. If a word could scream of its own accord, which one would it be? Curse words are too easy, they were made to be shouted, or passed off in as passive aggressive manner as possible. Zit is one. On the count of three, join me in shouting zit. Okay, one... two... three... ZIT! I was a letter Z in a dream once, it was a magical place to be, at the end, so I didn't have to keep getting up for the others to move into position. I would wave at A and A would snub me, because everybody/thing that comes first has that their-shit-don't stick or stink attitude. I wave anyway, trying my hardest to break A down. I then shout, "A is for arsehole, Buddy!" only for B to shout back, "Huh?" and I will have to reiterate what Letter I was aiming it at, "Not you B! A. A for arsehole." B replies, "But after you said Buddy, and the pronouncing of the word B, it had a heavy emphasis on the letter B, which is me! I prefer being called Bernard than buddy, so for future engagements call me..." – "SHUT THE FUCK UP BUDDY!" V for Veronica Verily Vast Vapid Voluptuous Venomous Vixen screamed at B for not Buddy but Bernard. I waved at A until he eventually sidled up to me, as the other letters held their own in the constant bickering, or having tender conversations, like Y, O, U giggling, knowing that when they were put together, they represented You. A said, "A doesn't like to be waved at, but A does like to have the upward triangle sign, signed at him." With that A buggered off, and from that day onward I never paid A much attention; well, I did, but not like I used to. Z didn't want to play into his A-hole non-hands, his A angular stepladder sides, games. I loved how agitated A got, because A had given me a sign to sign to As self, a meeting of two ends, given a rule to adhere to, and me being the end point, rebel, where I, Z, not actually I (I for Ianthe) can drop off and never return, and though A has that option, he never does, because A is a self-important A-hole, and has to stay in that superior position – I decided to witness his undoing, feeling empowered. A gave me a sign, that I should greet and approach A with the upward V sign, which I couldn't do, not well, as I was Z, but I wouldn't try, not for his amusement, and not to reinforce his delusions of grandeur. I made this last for nearly all of mankinds time, when they still used letters to communicate. On that final day A admitted in his A-holiness, and me, Z wrapped my lower rung around A and we walked off into the sunset, with X, Y trailing along, both gossiping as to how we as a trio would make it work. X said, "XAYZ?", but Y had other ideas. Y was going to bend A into submission. Until A was nothing but... a mere breath of an A-O! You will always think of faux pass (foe par) as FORX PASS! Fool. Irritant. Sod. Git. Muppet. Jerk. Asshole. Freak. Weirdo. Coffee fan. Instant coffee is good, kid, you know it to be true. Coffee snob snubber. Turkey leg grabber. Skinny leg jean wearer, showing the world your most athletic of body parts. Your gut isn't shoved into the waistband area, stretched beyond all logical proportions.

INTER-LEWD:

I am a life-sized toilet rim block. My function is to clean the gutters, the streets, the walls - every surface of reality with my thick blue ejections, that are only enabled by the bipolar weather. I don't want to neglect the fact that I must employ two illegal immigrants to carry me on their shoulders; as, how else would I be able to clean the streets without these two strapping carapaces bearing men carrying me about to fame and toilet industry misfortune?

SAVE US

Save the bees. Save the wasps. Save the planet. Save your souls. Save money. Save this child. Save this cat. Save this dog. Save this person who has lost their job. Save this. Save that. Save the ego of a trans-person who has lost a job because they do not agree with their bosses wayward antiquated views. Save things to your Wishlist. Save Greta Thunberg from being corrupted. Save your thumb from catching on the stove. Save your thoughts for another day. Save the messages from your ex all so you can look at them and obsess over their meanings years after they were sent. Save your firstborns' foreskin. Save the blotchy bread for bread-and-butter pudding. Save your coupons, they last longer. Save space for desert. Save space for the Saharan sandy dessert. Save deserted fighter pilots caught in a time loop. Save Christopher Nolan from going back to Warner Brothers pictures. Save Pixar from self-combustion. Save these words for later perusal. Save the religious fanatic from his own self. Save your grandmother the hurt of revealing that you identify as a wallflower and wish to contribute a beautiful, embossed pattern in her shitty one-bedroom flat on some murky council estate. Save cigarette butts and leave them in little anthill style piles for the shifty kid with a broken leg and a wonky left eye, who lives in a FOYER. Save the word Foyer and repeat it to someone in England and they will think it is a French word pronounced stupidly. Save this line, The Foyer movement in the UK developed in the early 1990s as a government sponsored response to inter-related youth problems of homelessness, unemployment and limited training and recreation facilities. Save it. Save it so you can decide when your kid play's up to send them there and ruin their lives. Save up enough money for your sagging tits and rolls of excess skin. Save the polluted pond all because you let your daughter watch The Simpsons Movie (2007) at an age where they are easily led, and now you have to stop at every cloudy pond to test it for pollution. Save these memories, especially the one where the ponds in your local areas were free of all forms of pollution and junk and had to piss in one a few blocks from your house all so your daughter could feel a little bit like that do-gooder Lisa Simpson, fucking yellow bitch! Save the saliva that you caught into a recycled glass Gü pot that streamed out of your mother as she ejected everything not asswards but mouthwards. Save the funeral flowers and press them into a POUNDLAND store diary. Save you aborted foetus you spat out of your grimy vagina hole. Save face when getting into an argument with deluded fucktards called Deluded Duncan and Lazy-Loopy-Lie-anna. Save the last line of cocaine for your friend who has travelled thousands of miles to watch you get frisky with his college crush, which is your own sister. Save all of your cinema tickets in a slippery fish and then delude yourself that any of these tickets have any meaning outside of your collectomaniac-self. Save the word collectomaniac to your Word document because it apparently isn't a word but save face and hit the ADD to Dictionary icon, I won't tell. Save the defenceless kid getting bullied by kids two years above him and don't feel bad for knocking out the little cunts, and ignore the police threatening you with this, that all the usual piggy threats, you know you done good, you crazy 79-year-old ex-conman. Save the wallet that you found of a tram in Praha, not to try find its owner but to delude yourself you have the balls enough to commit fraud and steal what little is in said wallet. Save the screenshots on your phone that prove you are being harassed, merely for the police to shrug, log it, do nothing, and make you feel seen, not heard, heard but not understood. Save the photo and later manipulate it. Save your favourite FREE AI Image Generator and feel nothing but freedom when getting beautiful images for your indie book. Save the indie scene by inverting it. Save your anus from prison daddies and in-denial cocksuckers. Save the phonebook that your grandfather used to flick through and highlight certain numbers only to forgot which page it was, even though you told him to either earmark the page or leave a different coloured post it note on said page that he needed, with directions and details written on the note pad, to better help him, then again, I think he liked to make a fuss, and then again, there is not enough colours to encompass and guide a mad phonebook, Yellow Pages flicker like you, old grandpawps. Save all of your grandmother's hardcover books released under the name James Patterson and get them piled into a great mountain in her front yard and as she suckles via her nostril tubes third-hand oxygen, as you can't afford cannister oxygen, only those you steal from the care home you work at as a porter, you set it alight, proud as punch, and all she does is shrug, only for you to realise that she didn't shrug, she fucking well died. Save the Micro Presses by donating to their PayPal, but don't be a punk-ass bitch and send it as anything but a gift, otherwise, you get taxed, you nasty fucker. Save the world by rebelling. Save the world by reading your written works, only to bore the tits off everyone in attendance. Save time and just self-publish. Save your life by not getting into anything artistic. Save toilet roll because we never know when Covid-20 will hit us, and you all know, it will hit us harder than last time. Save images of Trump, just so you remember that cunts do exist, and they do get into the Grand Oval office, on far too often a basis. Save me from myself. Save your memory on your phones, don't record this, I am a fat Brit pretending ting to be something he is not. Save this line, I am Zak Ferguson and you have been a delightfully patient and understanding audience. Save your breath. Save your claps I am not done yet, on stage, on tarmac, in book, in head, on the curled lip of Kenneth Anger, on the Kafka Shore Murakami wrote about, not that I read that book, so fuck knows why I am referring to it. Save this moment. Save the savor that my waffling produces. Save the day and just admit, you do not care about pronouns and just want to finish your dinner. Save yourself the worry, this isn't anti anything, it is anti-everything. Save the bath bubbles in some cheap Amazon purchased vial. Save it. Save it. Save it. Save the zit that didn't pop but just fell off your face, like a mollusc pried from a shifty crab back on the seafront of Peacehaven, some extension of the beach from Saltdean, that reaches to the Marina Harbour in Brighton. Save words. Save phrases. Save the legacy of Kathy Acker, because when Chris Kraus writes a memoir, oh boy, you sure as shit know that she couldn't care less about Acker. Save face.

Save full-frontal nudity in such places as these. Save the lady who dances and doesn't get the response she needs, that she deserves. Save RG Vasicek from me hugging him and getting my DNA all over his body, that he will no doubt transfer back to Queens New York and his wife will sniff, recoil, wave her hand about, asking him, "Why do you stink of sin?" Save the Armand philosophy, which is "I do not do NON-DISCLOSURE CONTRACTS," which I took to mean, fuck off you bastard, but it didn't, it meant come on fat boy, this isn't how true rogue operators, Rene's favourite phrase, works. Save David Vichnar from falling asleep manning the table with a beautiful selection of books. Save Vichnar the hassle of explaining why I am there or here, on page, in your presence. Save my books onto your Kindle, even though I don't put my books out on Kindle, and when I do, hahaha, yes, I wrote that and I will laugh that and read that out like some autogenerated sex-call centre bot, as it is released as print replica, take that you Kindle loving savants. Save your favourite flavoured fruit pastels. Save chocolate wrappers and frame them, reminding you that you eat far too much chocolat-tay! Save the big industries from crashing down. Save myself when I read or write that out, I am sorry, I am not meant to upset you reader, audience member, event ticket collector who is huffy and puffy as is. Save the serial killers numbers, so you can leave pervert-noise-breathing on their voicemail, knowing they'll never hear it, but some warden will, and he'll be wanking himself off thinking it's some fan girl clit-osising her right to want to fuck a sicko like, well, who is there left? Save the mints. Save the loose tile. Save it because it might be useful. Save your money. Save yourselves. Save the word conserve. Save the word protect. Save me from doing the most ludicrous thing, which will be asking the first lady who touches my arm politely to marry me off, no, not marry me, I am taken, to marry me off, which sounds kind of kinky, but it isn't, it is just a British way of mulching the English language. Save Praha from those scary rollercoasters outside, those scooters, no, no, I cannot go on one, it is too fast. Save me from my autistic not so fine motor skills. Save your energy, do not get up and buy my books, they are for free anyway, that is, if they reach Praha in time for an event, I am deluding myself I am coming to, when Vichnar and Lois haven't invited me or given an indication they want me within an arms distance of them both. Save my writing by reading it and then leaving a negative review on Goodreads. Save my manifesto, which comes in a 22 stone body. Save me. Save us. PLEASE JUST SAVE US!

PART II:

sparse

THE
QUESTIONER

Questioner asking questions to the questionee sequestering reality A and Reality Z.

Questioner: **What is your function?**

Questionee: To change the way our interview will be translated onto the page.

Questioner: **What is wrong with it?**

Questionee: Just look at it!

Questioner: **There is a distinction between the two.**

Questionee: I want to be italicized.

Questioner: **That can be done.**

Questionee: I also want you to be known as Q, and myself as A.

Questioner: **I don't think it works like that.**

Questionee: You are Q. I am Z.

Questioner: **Very well.**

Z: Perfecto!

Q: **Why did you include your attempt at mainstream science fiction, in the above pages?**

Z: I didn't. It is a purely science fictional piece, and nothing mainstream about it, sir.

Q: **I believe you put it into the mainframe of this book, at the latter stages, to prove something to your audience?**

Z: Maybe.

Q: **Did you want to reward the reader with something a little more graspable, bearable, and perhaps even narrative driven?**

Z: I think so.

Q: **Why?**

Z: Why ask why? Why is it always coming down to why? *Why-oh-why* can't you just ignore the w, h, y, and shape the question mark with your lips. Why doesn't need a question mark at the end, because why is a question, a word that pushes for an explanation, for a reason, and what does the question mark represent, no, I am not asking, as I don't need to ask because my facial expression and tone frames the mark, but I assume this needs to be implemented when transcribed to tell the audience what tone of voice and what supposition I am using.

Q: **Do you understand the English language?**

Z: No. Nor should anyone else. I believe Language is a form of virus. A virus that we all seem to struggle against, and feel the need to heal from, or immunize. How? By following the patterns that some silly bastard from the Mid-5th to 7th AD century felt compelled to do. What came before? Latin? Gibberonian? Click-clacking?   Language is weird. People are weirder. Language isn't there to teach, preach and to be used for dastardly sly devils. It is for experimenters.

Q: **Do you enjoy what you do?**

Z: I enjoy nothing. Life is awful. I hate life.

Q: **Do you feel that there is a romanticization with the tortured artist?**

Z: Of course, there is. All writers are egoists and sentimental, who believe their agony is greater than anybody else's.

Q: **Why do writers romanticize their agony?**

Z: It is a persona. An image. A place to create something apart from their truer selves.

Q: **Which is?**

...

    ...

        ...

Q: **Which is?**

...

    ...

        ...

Q: **Oh, I am sorry. I forgot to italicize you!**

Z: Thank you.

Q: **Back to my previous question. Which is?**

Z: Wait, let me respond, in italics, then you can ask your question, your response to my response… It is a persona. An image. A place to create something apart from their truer selves.

Q: **Which is?**

Z: They are boring lonely sad fuckers who outside of their work are nothing. I think this needs to be an essential and key component of being an artist.

Q: **How many books have you written?**

Z: Millions. I have just forgotten them, always writing them, composing them, directing them, filming them, painting them, between drifting off and the total collapse of consciousness.

Q: **I wish to extend this interview to your friends.**

Z: I have no friends. Nor enemies.

Q: **Fellow writers and artists then, that I know you champion and support.**

Z: Go for it. Bye.

Q: **This means you must ask them questions.**

Z: Me? Why me?

Q: **Because you are Q, as well as Z.**

Z: Well, fuck me backwards and call me Cecilia Aherne.

Sadly, the interviews could not be conducted, because Zak had a temper tantrum because Q would not supply Z/Zak with his very own conducting baton.

THE
WANDERING
MAN

The wandering man.

The wondering man.

The wandering-wondering man.

The wondering-wanderer.

The slump shouldered bloke you see in the distance in some field.

You never really give him much thought.

We often assume that he has a right to be there.

He is a wanderer, but only for a mere few minutes, until he reaches one of his farm animals.

We never see him with his animals.

Still, he is a famer... *why else is he out there come rain or shine?*

The wandering man is not wandering, going for a walk, not in our minds, spotting him, on the top deck of a double decking heading inward to Eastbourne.

We assign him a purpose.

He is not out there on his own as a lonely old bloke trying to combat his arthritis.

This supposed wandering man, he has a purpose.

Why would he be out in torrential rain, hands sunk into his front pockets, head bowed down, fighting the wind for the mere sake of wandering?

We think so many thoughts, within a blink of the eye.

Then, it is lost.

The wandering man will not be thought upon until you next see him or somebody that resembles him.

The wandering fellow has no part to play.

In reality.

He wanders.

Determinedly forcing his way onward.

Is that wandering?

No.

It can't be.

He is the Purposefully Striding Man.

No.

No, no, no, no!

He is and always shall be a wandering man.

What else is there to add.

No more, no less, little detail can be added to his character, his shape, his whole existence.

He wanders.

Then, you see him... if it is the same bloke, again, and the same questions repeat themselves, only a little different, residing in your subconscious, needing a certain ingredient to make it bloom in time lapsed dough to bread baked fashion – it feels weighty and fuller.

It is extending off from where you last left off when you (thought) you last saw him. Until he greets a lamb with a violent tug, smelling its wool and envisioning the first shear of its existence, and its later life, warming his stomach and bloating him.

Then it is gone.

Rain within rain.

Tears unto rain drops.

Raindrops obliterated by spherical teardrops.

A fart in the wind.

A fart in a mason jar.

A fart cupped in Sylvia Plath's palms, warming her up in the coldest of nights.

A fart that left to its own devices in a workspace makes everyone gag and fan it away; only encouraging it on its everlasting stomach churning, gag-reflex triggering journey of gaseous discovery.

A fart that Peter Jackson withheld for so long, when he unleashed it he lost ten stone; only to put it back on when back to making J.R.R Tolkien adaptations.

Just because he is in a field, and with a wool-lined coat and old geezer cap on, he must be a farmer.

He isn't.

He only looks to be determinedly fighting the elements.

He is a mere wanderer.

The wanderer wanders because wandering induces wonderment.

He touches the air.

He manipulates it.

He doesn't make a dog and pony show of his advances in his human guise.

He just toys with it.

He toys with the imagery surrounding him.

Reality is his virtual reality.

He can alter, shift, block, angle, shift, break, stop, pause, speed, reverse everything around him.

The wanderer decides not to.

Why?

Because it isn't in his nature to play God, when he doesn't believe in any deities apart from his own self.

If an imagined, superior being, altered throughout the centuries can have almighty power, in fictional terms passed off as real, then a man with such power doesn't need to harness it.

He can just recognise it in his own time and continue wandering.

The man wonders sometimes about when he started wandering.

As soon as that thought enters his mind, it wanders off as vapours from his nostrils and mouth.

LET ME
TELL YOU

Let me tell you... I was born with an innate skill for remembering film lines, film scenes, and at the same time, unable to verbalise them. All I could do was make noises; noises that concretized the term spastic.

Let me tell you... I hate myself. I hate my body. My voice. My writing. The only part of me that is good is hidden somewhere in my past.

Let me tell you... I do not deserve Laura-Jane Marshall.

Let me tell you... I think my trauma has been written about enough, so much so, that it really bores me too.

Let me tell you... I have never had sex with a man. Do I want to? Well, curiosity killed the cat, but that was only because he had one life left.

Let me tell you... if you have managed to get this far, you really deserve your money back. Which I am not at liberty to do or try and achieve.

Let me tell you... Writing like mine, it has no role in the literary hierarchy beyond making a valid point. A point of making something out of nothing. There is an art in unartful gesticulating.

Let me tell you... I take nut-nut pills.

Let me tell you... The nut-nut pills make me hungry, and they make sure this tub of lard can actually go sleepy night-night!

Let me tell you... My staying up late really fucking annoys my fiancée.

Let me tell you... I once punched a kid in the face. I was a kid as well.

Let me tell you... I hung a kid out of the top floor window of a FOYER because he was a rape-y sonavabitch!

Let me tell you... I sired a kid with a monster.

Let me tell you... the owls are what they seem, and they want their upstanding reputation back, thank you very much Mr. Lynch!

Let me tell you... Those goo-goo-gaga people that believed Gaga had a penis, they masturbate religiously over that freezeframe shot in Bradley Cooper's brilliant film A STAR IS BORN.

Let me tell you... Gaga fucks like a maniac! I don't know from experience, but everyone she co-stars with, she is overly familiar and sexual, and you can tell her way is mind fuckery.

Let me tell you... Lady Gaga is a reg flag I'd love to wave!

Let me tell you... Dennis Cooper is a beautiful human, and I might be falling in love with him. Don't tell Laura.

Let me tell you... I mention Dennis Cooper because I like-like him, so, so much.

Let me tell you... Once Upon a time Zak Ferguson used to smell of weed when he sweated a lot.

Let me tell you... He now smells like a stale, out of touch with modern tastes Willy Wonka not-so-chocolate-based factory.

Let me tell you, that blue line that keeps appearing is pissing me off!

Let me show you...

Let me tell you... Once Upon a time Zak Ferguson used to smell of weed when he sweated a lot.

Let me tell you... you have one hundred pages more of this nonsense.

GWEN-TEN

(lyrics)

Quen-TEN! the two of us need look no farther

We both recovered what we were eyeing up

Like a blondes delicate feet

Oh, QUEN-TEN!

Beat your rubbery Planet Terror goopy meat

With an acquaintance to telephone call my own

I'll no way be alone

And you, my QUEN-TEN! will see

You've got a mate in me

(You've got a friend in me)

Ben, you're always running here and there (here and there)

You feel you're not wanted anywhere (anywhere)

If you ever look in front

You can have a big Hollywood lunch

With Quentin!

And don't if yah like what you can't video store find

There's something you should buy

A life!

Like Ben-10s,

That of a Quen-Ten!

You've got a spot to go

(You've got a rowboat to repo)

I used to say "Yuck" and "Hee-hee"

Now it's "blanket", now it's "pronouns he not she"

(I used to say "blanket" and you said "Daddy, I wanna spank it")

(Now it's "Micheal-me", now it's "we-hee-hee")

Ben, Ten, Quent, Ten, truly people would turn you gay

(turn you gaaaaaaaaaaaaay, for a moment a daaaaaaay)

I don't listen to a name they say (a weird Neverland free tour today, they say, they say, oh, hee-hee, they say)

They don't see much of my real complexion, as I do in my gas chamber lid reflection

I hope they cry, try to

Get Ben, in bed, all so Quen-Ten can film a freshly bobbed bitches numb digits,

I'm sure they'd think on their Rotten Tomatoes scores, again

If they had a companion like Ben-10

(A buddy)

Like Ben-10

Only it is pronounced, GWEN-TEN!

(Like Ben-10)

Like Ben-10, only with Quentin.

- Michale Jack Sohm

YOUR

Your stomach is cramping, making the mind convulse as violently as your abdomen.

Your feelings towards another man in the most heteronormative ways has gone unrequited.

Your dancing skills can be extricated metaphysically as well as physically.

Yours for mine.

Your child needs to get a grip.

Your dog shit on my yard, so either you go pick it up, and write ten long pages that declare, MY DOG WILL NOT SHIT ON YOUR YARD AGAIN, or I will nut you in the noggin, and televise it for the world to laugh at/with.

Your time machine keeps making the oddest of noises, and as I cannot process noise like anyone else, I feel it in my fingers, I cannot feel in my toes, the time-machine around us, seems to emanate an angry glow.

Your timepiece says it is 7:00am but you feel like it is 8:00am, and as perverse as this may all seem, at the end of the day, do not eat breakfast without a morning juju-hit!

Your mind is telling you, yes, but your body, yes, your obese body is saying no, no, no, no, no, no, no.

Your past creeps up on you, and taps you on the shoulder, and no matter how fast and slick toed you are you can never face it head on.

Your shorts are too tight, I can see your male camel toe from here, and it for sure looks greasy Mr. Taliard.

Your infatuation with me would be a bashful
thing if you were anyone else but your dogged,
junky self.

Your first love has died; people keep asking you, how do you feel? You respond by saying, you're your own worst enemy when you ask such a rude question; how can I feel, when I never even pecked her on her sweet not-so-rosy cheeks?

Your car has been interrupting your train of thoughts because that is what vehicles do; they make sounds to drive you to the edge of insanity; or what you consider your short fuse, that, depending on the offending person or thing, can be extrapolated in various ways - and your expertly WORD documented and graphed "thin-line" between sanity and insanity is made null and void. Yet, it is closing in, the car is juddering, spitting grit, plastered with wet leaves, crusty bird-shit spray that has been baked onto the car's hood like some ancient paper mâché version of whatever *Azathoth* is meant to be, where insanity is pointed at by crowds and miscreants. Insanity pushed into your temples, devil horns being so 1920s, the insanity fashionists cook up some hasty plan for all on the cusp of insanity temple throbbers to sprout horns of deer, topped off with, leaking, oozing, Brussel sprouts which means, you were never really sane to begin with.

Your interviewing skills leave a lot to be desired, when you know the desirable part of you was lost with the Titanic, you time travelling fool.

Your right hand has twisted and created a shape that resembles the left.

Your left hand has mangled itself to replicate the right hand, which is trying to mimic the left hand, so it is a subversion upon a subversion, and has inadvertently created a hand (timey-wimey or is it winey?) loop that distorts timelines and planetary orbits.

Your meant to be sleeping, dear one, "But Mum, I am eighteen years old, stop tucking me in like I am eighteen months old."

Your always saying bless you to me, when I haven't finished sneezing, and it really fucks me off.

Your human, so when you sleep, you start talking to yourself, then realise that it is your fifteenth personality speaking to your twenty-fourth personality.

Your mirror reflects various personalities who have left a deep impact on your sordid little life.

Your isn't You're; get it right, sheesh! - but you
are a fan of hating on weird literature.

Your best mate is not really reading this, whilst you can at least admit to casually acknowledging it, though you are skimming this.

Your picking lemons and decide to become a lemon that'll be used to lighten the lamb dish.

Your car is ready to end its vehicle life.

PART III:

the end before the end

YOU'RE

You're not right in the head.

You're not left in your head.

You're Evil.

You're intoxicated.

You're a thought left to modify all surrounding externalia.

You're a fraud.

You're fractious.

You're beaten.

You're a film critic with no newspaper to run your reviews.

You're regretting all the books you shoved out,
because too much means too little.

You're a little ant under a microscope, fighting the heat.

You're an ant-bully.

You're a cat kicker.

You're a dog shooter.

You're a poet in disguise as an experimenter.

You're a faux pass.

You're a degenerate scum bum from Scotland or Ireland or Brighton or New York. You're an article hound. You're an internet abuser.

You're a clown with no makeup left for your grand finale.

You're Russel T. Davies writing Doctor Who on a deadline, trying not to explode at Christopher's awful comments.

You're a film director with no experience with lenses or cameras or rigging or lighting, or anything that a director should know.

You're coming to the end of, whatever this thing was/has been/will be.

You're entering words into the prompter and the prompter is prompting you with the four images, each extremely square – images it creates by hacking, splicing, recreating artwork in the style of ad-infinitum...

You're wounded. You're scared. You're obsessive. You're a freak of nature. Nature is freakish, but that doesn't mean by osmosis that you are the embodiment of all its inarticulate parts, does it? You're smiling, because I have said and used a word that you do not know, and with the tone of our embrace, our words left to hang and interknit, to combine, to pair us as one functioning tendril of experience, you feel safe, that I used a word that you have never heard, and would never have used, even if you did know it and how best to fashion it into a sentence and conversation; by not knowing if the word delivers, in how it is framed, you still understand the intent behind it; the severity of the word; even though to do not know if it makes sense in the context that it is used in, you accept it, and like the speaker of that word (which was it, osmosis?) you feel seen, heard, and of course embraced.

You're a whistleblower. Not a whistleblower in the sense of you take inside secrets and blow the lid right fucking off – so extreme a projectile you knock out the three reaming teeth of your grandma. You appreciate a whistle. All whistles. You do have a favourite though. You love the weenie whistle. You sit under stranger's windows, and blow. Not long and hard, as the weenie whistle is a sensitive plastic object. You stifle your giggles as they look first through a crack in the curtains or blinds, and you continue, whether you know they are being alerted to your whistleblowing antics, you plough onwards with your weenie whistling. Sometimes they catch you, but as you're so small, dressed in clothing only a lonely country boy would dare be seen in, they take not umbrage, but a sympathetic expression. Though there was that one time you blew on the hard, brutal storm whistle you had bid on for months and months until finally the eBay seller of said storm whistle gave in, to your slow increments of, not pounds, but cents – and there was no initial curious window peeping, the old bloke almost torn the window from its hinges, grabbed you by your collar, pulled you into the room you were seated beneath, knees tucked under your chin and forced to suck, not his toes, but his wife who he told you was in a state of paralysis because of the constant whistleblowing. You argued this was the first time you had whistle blown in this region, but he wouldn't hear of it; he made excuses for every counter argument you had. You sucked on her toes and brought her back into reality. She then started to produce her own whistles too. It all seemed rather kosher, and expected, as you felt it was an eventuality that you'd fuck with the wrong people at some point, and they'd make you suffer for your whistleblowing actions, so you took it in your stride; you didn't really think on it much when you made your way back home, rubbing your tongue on the roof of your mouth, enjoying the aftertaste of her fine feet, smearing it in your maw – when your other half asked why you had "what looks like…" cum, dried on your fleece jumper. *Mea culpa*. You're a fan of teleprompters, as you love the analogue and the modern converging and making sweet, sweet commercial newscasting event hosting and line delivering *luvva-luvva*. You're tired of being fatigued. You're tired of the tirelessly determined exhaustion that you can only manage to describe as "tu-tu-ter-ired!" – that haunts your bones, brain, and especially your sense of place. You're an indie writer asking another indie writer if they'; blurb your book, in hope that their audience might pick up your own, and we all know blurbs are a deliverance of approval, that we can use to market and sell. You're honest enough with yourself to know that it will not work. You're entering a matrix designed by a fourteen-year-old prodigy; sorry, The Prodigy fan. You're nearing a point in your life that you wish to take a photo of whatever form it comes in and print the "photograph" digitally captured image out at one of those self-service desks in your local Pharmacy and BOOTS (Boots UK Limited (formerly Boots the Chemists), trading as Boots, is a British health and beauty retailer and pharmacy chain in the United Kingdom. It also operates internationally, including Ireland, Italy, Norway, the Netherlands, Malta, Thailand, and Indonesia.) forgetting, in quotation marks, to pay. You're aware of being hyperaware, whilst everyone else isn't as hyperaware as you make yourself, though you have a degenerative disease called impatience. You're a gestalt. You're corrupted. You're hippy. You're punk. You're a magician without a bunny-rabbit in the hat, as that rabbit died long, long ago, in a dusty theatre in Croydon. You're reading this not as you, but as me, when I want the I in yourself to be encompassed. You're the book. You're these words. You're the narrative. You're the story dear reader, you are the author. You're the person that illuminates these linguistical shapes and forms that make a dyslexic weep over. You're not only dyslexic you're also a bloody fool, for having taken my hand when I offered it to you. You're now being stink palmed by this book. Embalmed by my shitty underwear. You're not taking full advantage of the fact that I have written these incantations for you to read aloud. This book needs to be read aloud, otherwise the prose will be criticised for that of which it is not at all trying to pass itself off as; which is? Decent prose. Decent verse. Decent editorial savvy bequeathed unto its digital self; a dirge, a dirge I tell you, a dirge against all common sense. You're attracted to experimental works because they are usually just images on a page, delivered via typographical manipulations, and processed as word sludge, I hate the phrase WORD SALAD, who wants to eat a salad with words in it? – easier to log on Goodreads, ticking off another number, adding to your reading goal. You're on Facebook, and you spot a post by me, and it reads: No one cares. Which means, I am, or have been doing something right. You're left contemplating it; how should you respond, or whether you should respond at all. You're getting ready for the Christmas period. Gushing reds and sickly greens, it resembles Ginger Lynns cootchie-coo-cunt. You're Wish listing your wants and needs on Amazon. A need isn't the same as a want. Well, it sure is in our day and age, amiright? (High five me!) No, no high five. Shame. You're not bored. You're in the process of transcending boredom. Meaning?

You're awake. You're alert. You're vigilant. You're Batman without the eye makeup. You're James Wan moving onto the next project, annoyed at how long his billion-dollar earning Aquaman films' sequel took to be... released. You're Liam Neeson in silly clothes screaming, "RELEASE THE KRAKKEN!" and each time you do a squid dies peacefully before being gobbled down by a Korean squid connoisseur. You're thinking a thought that you assume I have rattling through my mind; have you ever asked whether you should before you actually do? No. I do as I please. You're cutting the leg of lamb poorly, and there are crunchy edges to your slices that weren't there before you started plating the cuts up. You're reading these words, and I hope you are mouthing them. You're willing to, so why not do it.? You're remembering a moment in time when you were in the library and picked up a book ,started reading, you're uncertain you can manage a book like this, so, to help ease your expanding literacy skills a chocolate covered, blonde haired, psychotic eyed four-year-old starts to publicly shame you for "Speaking whilst he is reading, mummy why is he reading whilst speaking!" – so you stop. You're left thinking about that kid, and his eyes, and come to the conclusion that anyone with eyes like that is going to grow up into one mean-spirited, bully boyish uneducated cunt.

PART IV:

Another voice from the margins

This is a script.

Read your lines.

<u>Silently</u>.

<u>Internalise</u> it.

<u>Then</u> act it out.

Go for it!

Here are your lines, and I do not want to direct you, you have full control over how these lines are spoken aloud and shared.

Just be warned, the words are harsh, angry, vengeful, and even though there is no indicator of where or what this character has gone through; their upbringing or geographical location, you can just tell that these words have been written with the intent of being spoken with a Boston accent — it is just the nature of the Bostonian — when you write an angry American character that is what the words will automatically assume themselves as.

Ready.

Go for it.

ACTION!

YOU THINK, YOU THINK THAT YOU FUCKING OWN ME!

NO ONE OWNS ME!

I OWE YOU NOTHING.

MY SALIVA IS BOILING INFO WARS AND

SCALDING SEXUAL DISEASES and the WATER I SUPPLY YOU IS ACID FROM

THE GUTS OF A HARLEQUINN AND HER RUGRET FUCKING SPAWN!

Do I sound like I'm on the medication?

No, fuck you, fuck that, like fuck am I!

This rare weed I smoke is holistic in all its green splendour.

I do not need your placebos you lying faggots of commerce.

Fucking meatball and gravy meal slurpers.

We've been told for too long that the pills ignite something inside ourselves.

We are conned into a false sense of security.

These pills, their dispensers, their cult, their holy message men, and caterers.

I'll burn them all.

I have nothing left to lose.

Fuck this.

My one ally is now drooling her slop back into her Parkinson-assisted bowl, surrounded by some fucking climbing frame, fed back to her as a new meal.

Like, what the cunting fuck?

My money pays for three meals, not one meal reheated over and over.

Liars.

You have ostracized society.

You surgeons of fatigue and placebo.

She had to die.

Bang!

One finger still inside her. I felt her warmth escape through her slick... cunt ... you took my life and love from me...you took too many of us from our second-hand thrift store bought typewriters that didn't FUCKING WORK!

CUNTS!

She decided to blow buckshot into her fucking eye in hope something would give.

Instead she is looking like some painting by some British queen who loved bad boys and wine.

"Cheerio!" should be Francis Bacon's one AND ONLY quote.

Nothing would give.

At all!

That's why she had to die.

This isn't paranoia because I HAVEN'T ASCRIBED NOR SUBSCRIBED TO YOUR DOCTRINE.

Her cunt dried up.

Her lubrication fetish dried out too.

I am at a loss what to do.

Kick-start my car, grab the hose pipe and funnel, the gaffer tape, doing everything to get high without losing my wages for some backstreet shyster selling me Norwegian Brown.

I was Colombian Spray.

The Powder of Nosferatu's retarded wives who got too close to the...sun.

I'm waiting.

Biding my time.

You all will succumb to this mania.

You see, this mania and anger is what came from your sultry ways and fancy dressage and furnishing of this big pharma universe.

I feel like I'm in a Todd McFarlane reality.

Promised everything and ultimately, given nothing but promises.

That's what the pill popping is all about.

I'm Derek Varence and I'm ready to blow this fucking thing wide open.

Not with hash-tagging this on Twitter or bitching on FuckBook, I'm literally going to blow this thing apart.

At the heart.

Inner city.

Inner universe.

Watch as all your pills fire out to the night sky like fucking whiz bangers and cheap corner store bought fireworks.

I'm ready big pharma, are you?

I've cooled off, and I've written out my manifesto in bullet point precision.

It is going to happen.

I have been stopping and starting my rundown Ford Dodge.

The rust comes away from the door even by looking at it.

I have scouted.

I have planned.

I am ready.

To do what is right and just.

I'm not going to research my American commandments.

No.

I need no excuse.

I'm this world's vigilante.

I am no Batman.

More a steroided pimp version of Robin.

With Bane's cock, as an additional appendage.

The excretion of a bloated God will rain down on New York and sizzle like gelatine-injected weenies on a fire pit.

All over New York.

The bug-eyed, cocaine destroyed nostrils, N Y C will be the first to go up, then down, in flames and rubble.

Acid rain.

Nuclear fallout from their triangulated fucked up psychogeographic symbols and architecture, that Alan Moore hasn't yet constructed to convince the world that Jack the Ripper is a Trans-sexual who goes by the name Grant Morrison.

Their empire is built out of super empirical, phallic structures.

What's new?

Huh, kids, ladies, and gentlemen?

What is new?

The glass and chrome are there to reflect our faces.

Chris Nolan is behind you, conning you that Inception isn't a Nightmare in Elm Street rip-off.

Entropy is cool.

I wish only this could be attained.

Not by the facsimile version of Denzel, but the legit Washington.

This glass cock and small dick tugger, extender, this delusion is infallible.

Reflecting the status quo.

The benign cancers we are for ourselves and to each other.

To disturb our sense of self.

This big building can be you, so go inside, jerk off over the receptionist, maybe think on blowing it up.

Impregnate her and go underground, and binge watch Uwe Boll films.

These things are there to crumble.

To fall into themselves.

Even Uwe Bolls restaurants.

When I blow shit up, I want it to feel deliberate, structured, prepared, and clean.

The symmetry is a new high.

The dope doesn't cut it anymore.

All these videos on YouTube and some Ezra Miller sounding they or them spazzoid narrating... they ruin the footage with their narration; subtitles used on the footage as watermarks.

I want the end of all end times to be micromanaged by myself.

I've been talking to a guy in the UK, seems fucked up enough to believe we can do this ourselves.

He is the fall guy.

A necessary means to a necessary end, a pulp character, plump, like an overfed Nick Park Chicken Run chicken - a big old chess piece, one given as much affection and attention it needs, to ensure it can be sacrificed...as if the bug-eyed Anya Taylor Joy is leaning over him/it... her slowly shrinking tits not giving off that scent we wanted, that alure.

This is 2019s Anya, not 2000 and twenty fucking three's Anaya. Not so much Taylor Joy.

The eyes get bigger, and the tits get flatter.

What little fat she had, is slowly shrinking away into nothing.

Fuck that and fuck you.

Big pharma is using humanity as their watermark.

Cunts.

The word cunt fascinates me, as we Americans seem to toe curl over it, weep, easily triggered whereas in some backwater British towns, it's a term of familial endearment or mere joshing.

American swine, easily triggered, the pill munchers, so affected, so, so much we must fork out for their toenails to be removed from the heels of their cracked feet.

I hate you.

I hate them.

I hate big pharma.

Days have passed.

Things have been done.

Things that needed to be seen to.

IT IS DONE MOTHERFUCKER, WHY CAN'T YOU GET THAT THROUGH YOUR SKULLFUCKING SHAFT-LIKE HEAD!

Fuck, they've followed me for days.

They've found me.

They are somehow clued in... to my plan.

This is fucked.

What is going to happen, I do not know.

I am scared for my life.

THEY GOT ME. I KNEW IT WAS GOING TO HAPPEN. THEY GOT ME ENSNARED.

The sick fucks are playing the latest news report, on a loop, reporting that I was a terrorist who blew himself away in preparation.

This shit that they write, edit, and assign for those asshat fake tanned dopes to deliver in that monotone drone, it makes my ass burp and my mouth fart.

I'd blame the pills if news reporters or casters didn't exist before this global plague.

They delude themselves and the nation into accepting this as divine truth.

There is only one divine for me, and she chomped down on dog shit like a pro.

Brainwashing them with a silhouetted image, giving my name... my fucking name.

Apparently, I am a terrorist.

Fuck, give me a chance.

I hadn't even decided on which Big Pee I wanted to target.

I wonder how my Brit friend is faring?

You reply to Derek Vance, at a distance.

You write about him in the third person.

You write:

The news is that Derek Vance was a terrorist. I'm shocked to find out the news of his demise. To hit the news in the UK like it did, I felt scared that maybe he went ahead and did it all on his own... The destruction of big pharma? No, he only got caught in the act of inaction. Bleeding fool, I said. Fucking idiot...then I cried. I wept. I called my mother who has dementia and she comforted me as if she were an agony aunt, and not the woman who birthed and reared me. Derek. What the fuck happened? What did you do? We met online. Me and Derek. We were both deluded, pathetic louts with too much free time on their hands, oh no, no, no, no. My friendship wasn't based on two basement dwellers, posing as informants or insiders to the way things are run by big pharma. We were not like those morons, those incels of old.

We were not theoretical, nor saw ourselves as philosophers of the numbed age. We were realists. Collectors of prescriptions. We seemed to be the only two who knew what was really going on. We were witnesses to the end of the world. We, the inheritors of the new wave of consciousness. A mere realisation set us apart. We saw that we could retaliate. Seems he had his chance and blew it. Then again, who am I to be so judgmental? I wouldn't have been so blatant and bold in the face of Big Pharma like he was. I was just into this conversation, the potential of where it led. To bring down the establishment. Mere whimsy. Mere fantasy. It was fun, whilst it lasted. We lived in Squalor. It fit the image we had concocted. Between ourselves. United by strong band width and lined up time zones of communicada. It was a bond. A sealant on our loneliness for the time being. We slept with duvets made of scratchy pharma bags. Meds bags. Receipts. Everything we kept. We reused. From the outside looking in, these pills, this medication, that medication, this Pharma Weird intrusion was as much our reality as the peeping Tom's own. But it wasn't. (Sigh) This is a joke. Who am I kidding? I'm nothing without Derek. His life ended so suddenly and reached us, oddly enough, vis our news outlets. This has left me paranoid. It hasn't made me paranoid. I was paranoid before the news of his death, hence our union. A paranoid is only as fucked up as the subject matter they're so taken, possessed, and obsessed by. I've cleared out all evidence of our union and plan. I'm sorry, Derek, you're dead, and I am too weak to go to it all on my own. I'm scared. What if I am next? My body is no longer capable of revolting. My mind is, between 12am and 4am...where in the morning, I am at my most caffeinated and hyped, typing away carelessly on social media. Without a sounding board, it hits decaled walls and is lost between the cracks. Soaked up. No rebound and solicitation. Silence. Silencio. Derek wouldn't be so cowardly, like me, and he was the type who probably would have kept his loves dead body if he could. His love. His one love. Dead. Due to the pills and the people, the machines, the societal influx, the way we have turned autonomous and glib, the way Big Pharma lives on in us. We are all inexplicably pharma. Not big, the small parts. The cogs. The pistons. The switches. The electrical current is driving it into motion. He had, I mean to say, we had proof. Proof of this silent invasion. A professor of some renown agreed with us. She was silenced. We had proof. She had proof. Now, only I have proof. I made sure to lose it. Long lonely drives, scattering all evidence. Here. There. Every-fucking-where. Memories elongated like time lapsed roads; perspectives stretched. I'm untethered. I'm unmoored. I am adrift. I am dangerous. I am vulnerable. I am them. They are me. We are all big pharma. It can't be. The proof. Proof of what was really going on. It's in the pudding. Proof is in the pudding. On TV, Derek wasn't given a face. Just some clip art of a silhouette of a man... Scaramouche, scaramouche, can you do the big pharma fandango. Thunderbolt and pharma approved lightening, very, very frightening, yeeee gods who is Galileo, Galileo this is fucking wrong. He was painted for us, in all that media grubby journalistic blandness, in those awful tones, and their weird jittery broadcasting palette, the one *oh* one types of colours used, Derek, marked, spot lit as a villain, undeserving of recognition. Well played big pharma, well bloody played. 56 seconds worth of news. Was that all my friend Derek deserved? As I walk to collect my latest prescription, I happen to seize up. All my muscles are solid. I'm not a Greek statue, just a man, just a form, just a pawn, left posing nonchalantly in the middle of the street. I go down to get my pills. I look over at Tesco, and the shape, the dimensions are layered like colour burnt stock films. Everything is taking on a full tonto perspective. Maybe I need the pills. Yes, maybe I do. Derek had been my replacement. Maybe it's time to swallow...

Derek replied, Fuck you. Arnie you okay, you okay Arnie?

The Beach
of the
In-between

We were once told that we could achieve our dreams. Reach out our hands and pluck the stars from the sky. I wanted to do that and so much more. Our mission is top secret, but, like all great secrets, like the great Colonel, that finger licking chicken will be shared with the masses, - on the sly or for a cut. The training was touted to be easy, a breeze for chumps like me and co-pilot, but what is easy about any of this spaceflight? Nothing. It is a drag, like when we were kids and after the hundredth threat of an ass-spanking for not coming out of the sandpit when asked to leave, Daddio or Mommio come humiliate us in front of our supposed pals. Kicking up sand, grit, and dog shit, we are put through misery for having dared say, no. We dared not show our fatigue. We dare not show signs of giving in. There was no, NO in NASA. The hours are long, and the harsh mental probes lodged into our cortexes are even harder. BUT that isn't made public. Fuck man, what it means to pass every single test and challenge and be faced with recording one's inner thoughts. All I want is to hit the sack or pester my wife, knowing I'll be far away, from our universe. I'm going to space. This is nuts. Everything is going smoothly. Then the dreams started. The patterns. The sweats. It may be excitement. It might be, well, predestination come calling. The dreams when not experienced unconscious visit me at those most inopportune times. It isn't a signal of my mental decay. It is something else. The weaves of the universe are sending me a message. I took this as a sign that our goal would be achieved. Contact with them. The long walk to our shuttle. The walk of the soon to be heroes and pioneers. The walk of the damned. I can't tell you whether this is now thought as translated through a recording device implanted in my head, paranoia a-swirl, or I am dictating from a dislocated point in the unknown reaches of the universe. I am stuck. In this wonderful liquid, pebble-strewn void, where the intangible is made material and inter-real. Am I stuck or am I evolving? Am I human? Am I other? Am I pebble? Am I foam? Am I beach? Am I a corroded data dump? Processed as a robotic voice, for all my fellow space pioneers below to critique and pass between the board, before redacting all signs that the previously mentioned paranoia was a sign they should have picked up on before the shuttle was launched. Who knows? Who cares? I am witnessing the faces of the other. In these gateway portals. I am the hyperactive star streaks. I am no man nor machine. I am a celestial. I awake to find I'm a lens for the other side. My crew and shuttle are nowhere to be found. I am lost. I am dead. I am the messenger. Was this all deliberate? I was sent here to collect and send out ripples of data many zillions of miles away from my planet. That isn't a question. It's a reality. I am within. I am a progenitor. I am a creator. I am a God. No end to the beach. To that horizon. The implant must be disconnected if it hasn't been already. These are the last words, or the last impression of words unspoken from myself...God.

HEMMED

in by

ENERGY

Hemmed in by the abandoned cars psychosexual perverts on all sides, blood and hysterical laughter mingled with dissenting voices coming from the FM-SWEATBOX. Open to make sound more authentic. Ambient street. Odd Ambulance-shrieking towards that unnecessary car radio. Part of the raging acoustic surf, splintering arts, the damned smoking rubble of a dockside warehouse. EEG and a couple of weeks later when his energy returned there was still some lingering problems, he occasionally forgot rare diseases or surgical memory problems. A dozen years later life had returned to normal when suddenly there was this insatiable desire to buy recordings and became especially enamoured of a B-flat Minor Scherzo. I had the desire to play all the sheet babysitters, so now, just when I craved one, a nice little upright. I started to teach myself the few boyhood fingers on the heels of this sudden desire for his head. "The first time he said, it was in a dream...I was in something...I woke up startled...Still in my head...I jumped out of bed...started trying to write down a sort of reincarnation!" Transformed and given a special gift. A mission to metaphorically - with no breaks, no rests, to give it a shape and form. The seventh century Anglo Saxon poet, an uneducated goatherd fuck me who it was said fuck me had received fuck me the art of a fuck me dream. He spent the fuck me the rest of his life praising fuck me creation in hymns and fuck me harder poems. He got fuck me books on nothing fuck me-ings – this was a solitary pursuit – between himself and his fuck me now baby muse. He had experienced other fuck off and fuck me experiences since the strike. A new appreciation of, not fuck me and fuck you, but of art. Perhaps different fuck me tastes and fuck your new beliefs. Errrrrrrmmmmmmmmmmmmmmmmmmmmmmm mmmm you're not funny – he had become very spiritual since his near-death, his near-fuck-me-death, library of high voltage electricity he thought he could sometimes feel fuck me energy around people's fuck-me lightning bolt. Errrrrrrrrrrrrrrrrrrrrrrrrrrrrrrrrrrrrrrrrrrrrrrrrrrr rrrrrrrrrrrrrrrrmmmmmmmmmmmmmmmmmmm mmmmmmmmmmm some years passed, like they fucking do, new life...inspiration deserted him. He continued to work full time as a divorced motorcycle. He had no memory of Harley. And a period of convalescence to return to the surgery to change his motorcycle parts. Like dust, obsessive new cheerfulness was apparent in the same laboratory for fifteen years. Losing none of this professional sympathetic and living-it-up-a-bit, and a new fuck me love, a new fuck off passion, entered classical CDS into fuck me ports. Moved to Rapture or Tears, by special feelings, addicted to radio goo goo, which a colleague said, "Avoid your husband playing!" which she found irritating. This indifference to the patient was put on lamotrigine, the precise basis of their hazarded suggestion during years of incorrigible seizure activity and splashes. Might have developed an intensified functional connection between perceptual systems in the temporal lobes and parts of a limbic system involved an emotional connection that only became apparent when seizures were brought under control with medication. In the 1970s a sensory-limbic hyperconnexion might be the basis for the emergence of the unexpected sexual feelings that sometimes occur in people with wet willies and wet ears, and in people with temporal lobe near-death experiences and frontal lobe masturbation. An out of body experience both supernatural and mystical have arisen to a topic of neurological investigation for a century; relatively stereotyped in format. Tap dancing pixels and Morris gyrating temporal lobe sizzling's and evidence that both aspects of out of body experiences function alongside a altered state of being – transcendental – deaths and contained wanky-experiences, described by people in differed morse-codes and sext-messaging. Sagging tits spelling out the words njsdjknhgiuzdbdrhsjbnjjsd – sudden lightning best expressed as a common cardiac arrest – triggering basement dwelling shysters conning people on eBay. Neurological musicality. Sudden degeneration of the frontotemporal emergence of goats screaming for TikTok views and for decent grub. An emergent in tight elastic – bands looping around and around and around – abstraction in fashion-designer clutches and visions – language is key to everything and nothing. Lairs full of liars whispering to each other, confusing one lie with the next. Clearly this was not the case of the humble mutterer, secreted in the shrouds, hanging densely like theatre curtains, who is the narrator of all verses and prose. This was not the case of highly competent stroke damaging brains, living their lives after their owner popped his clogs. Consequently, it has all developed other problems, best surmised under macro fusion and intense sultry eyelash fluttering's. But there was nothing to suggest that disturbance of body illness can intensely consume a real dream or a wooden boy. Brain damage is a whole other plain to enter and decipher the glyphs of a sleepy mind. Consume a dream – these dreams that I have received over many years – donks upon donks of lusty-years. I have received many lightning conditions, hold the mayo, hold the mustard, with sudden vivacity, an unexpected creative passion/pattern. Creative passions. Sudden onset of fragments. Pieces. Parts. Dilutions. Arising from popular fragments –

TikTok'd and Instagram'd. Somewhat diffidently others, including professional commentators, with all their suggestions of growth – a strangely familiar seizure. A robust man started to get melodic, quite nice, soothing... vaguely familiar...There was an old, discarded electronic device in the speakers. Stillborns are blinded by a blizzard of cameras and illuminated phones. Fuck man! In those fondly recalled days of primitive systems regularly pulled for the crime of photographing the recording systems that were photographing the Checkpoint – dropping under the weight of weaponry, overwhelmed shuffling along with eyes down as if prospecting for dropped cops. Pigs go to bacon sizzle splash dynamic. Behaving like bouncers on grabbing minor celebs, throwing them into the party at the end of time. Groovy. Disco inferno. Dance with me, Dance with me, *Whoop-a-toot-woot!* *O, oh, o, oh, oh-o-oh-o*

White pages help get rid of mental discrepancies.

In focus the birds cohabit with their dead larder and creche. A ledge which frosted in droppings, this is the final colony from the Boris Johnson pigeon séance. Is that nobody challenges us, men poking a long rod under a rail, a rod with an attachment, a brutal flash, not flasher, conspiracy theorists blinded Princess Di's driver. Our surveillance city where image-making is always suspect, if not, fishing for pigeon portraits. Local matron on a string – never get rid of the bastards – I've lived here, and I've tried everything...they still frap on my foot...on the fucking place of all places...my cock. When we finished our day in the dark room, images flittering like pigeon wings, his camera on the end of an egg like crowns of heretic messiahs, subtle blues of metal. The domestic life of crannies under rails exerts a powerful twisting blade of the dick. Lightning strikes against the advice of its misdirected electronic gizmos and information overloads. To the core within, ice memories, in the blood, bricks made from the residue of the human waste. Smoke, shit. I remembered my fetish for tide-smoothed pieces of bricks. While you are just passing, dowsing a fruit, friends of the bicycle, a seventy-year-old black man dedicated Darwinism for the free breakfast. Because he's never aesthetically affronted terrible purple-skirts, hung dignified, to tell reveller's how to barbecue neck-tattoos on a wire-fence. The squeak of rubber on rubber, table tennis slabs, providing rough-sleepers and morning drinkers benches to congratulate each other on making it through on all sides. It has been promoted into a swishing black leotard, on your side coming in. Matching camouflage, side-by-side, the etiquette of survival, rattle towards shared portacabin colonies. Supporting between them with slim laptops within seconds they are forcibly on the edge of water. A nineteen-year-old, with no lunch, was a senior manager – though she's forty-seven, has she thought about, territorial imperatives. Mercenaries are frustrated by a floaty rattle trap – whispering assassins doesn't already give more texting and checking messages. Standing in the rubble. An alien invader taller than anything else in a bulbous plank-ribbed nest, an unfolded mass crushed into a space barely capable of tolerating its central section. It was under permanent scrutiny. With a fuck ton of Health & Safety issues. Enchanted in a suspension of grey dust. Through dim corridors we all search for the pre-war fingers – pickled in mason jars – others left out to dry – units and shelving keeping the Good Dr. Sheesha happy. Symmetrical stencilled graffiti – spray-paint disordered and running low low low low low. Images and tags from ankle dragging track suited plebs and their even more mongrel mong-meisters. 1968 walls covered in 2012 Olympic revolts and revolutionary visions. Stencilled plot points rubbed out by 89-year-old deary. Neighbourhood loyalties evolved around certain convenient flats dropped from the skies above. Better provoked soap, mingled with melting cheap store branded mozzarella. Soap bubbles pop on index-finger, held up like a bird has perched itself there. Pop gone popped! Deep folds of sentiment. Reflected faces in bubble sphere. Thinking perhaps of vagrant mainline stations – choo-choo, chug-a-chug-a-chugg! Breakfasting at The Vic. Moving onto the Tat, and then a fresh warm piss on the river Meath. 91 individuals witness his loose skinned foreskin. Manic penis. Half the audience check their phones but can't focus the cameras on his exposed slong. No topping up the bytes on their devices, it was time to read a book. 68 of them in unison…whip out their pocketbooks. Various literary classics. One pushed the penis revealer into the Meath. The place we called home, that we knew epitomised sin swallowed him down – due to the inversion he fell under the surface then came back up – rising higher and higher. Clouds swallowed him up like the inky depths of the Meath. He couldn't haul himself out of it…this event created a wave of suicides, spread through the 91 individuals like a Mexican wave at some rowdy football stadium. Deaths in red brick English stone dotted territories. A polished marker left to guide the territorialists. High up there was a 90-foot chimney stack. Used for coal-fired golden winds trapped and frozen into sculptures. What an odd thing it is to see billions of people playing with meaningless patterns – like plastic mould for children - dug out from scattered and uneven knolls of plastic construction blocks – the people preoccupied for much of their time, by what they call cerebral Overlords. Curiosity brings them back down to Earth's surface, to politely end the grand ingenuity initiative. While still finding the entire unintelligible spaceships rather complex. This thing called efficacious central human-water-boarding-simuls. Symbols are merely the stuff outsourced from greater materials, both foreign and regional, the stuff of language. The power of necessary rare overlords, appreciating tone or melodies created by burnt fuses – surrounded by fences, protective fences, some of these materials used on the mockingly named PRIVATE ROAD. The schoolkids were turned away at the time of the temporary closure and are now in their own secluded super-structure. A council block of ratty-tatty flats. From there they can control pitches and the guignol courts of Notserggah. They have purchased various extension scaffolding and a specific public realm. At the time of the closure, the estimated cost of renovation was small change, in light of the future projects. The council were in a hole looking for deals with private adventurers now turned into developers. So, they did what they always do, done best, they were economical, with the truth, and the spend-starship-thrift. With campaigners to take the heat out of protest – by putting energies into promises. A lottery-heavy grand project. Many things on the horizon. Witness the witnesses witnessing something witness-worthy. There was a building in a desolate spot, in the wrong place and at the wrong time. Wrong time, wrong place. The critic of Universal-Studies and Pop-Culture-Mic-Drops Jonathan Granc was no longer human. He was a pattern rotoscoped onto a 1960 alleyway wall. A pattern repeated so many times, through education and social services: the appointment of high-salaried advisers from Mars. CGI airport-dusk styles that fit a trend. That fits the Wrong Place, Wrong Time, building block. From their glass walls and concrete platters drilled into place by agitated Benefit-Bums, cracks appeared and out bled council-tax directives and numbers. From warped floors came out anxious, broken necked budgies. The overall budget of this block bled out also. The budget was out. Closed for remediation. Opened again. Stacked up the sheets of the Health & Safety issues redacted, scribbled, sufficiently evolved from a resolve – to allow the amenity in expressions of interest from man of the arts, which may have function. Maybe no function at all. They may be the byproducts of other motivational systems that give us an experience – that signals forms to correlate with sex – information-rich with data and concentrated powers. Made possible by using brain systems, that have been developed already for the involvement of a dozen scattered networks throughout the vexed, nonadaptive – exaptation's, a clear example, probably something similar in aspects of our higher aesthetic and intellectual life. Having entered the mind by "the back." Regardless of all this - the extent to which human powers and susceptibilities are hardwired. Or are a byproduct of proclivities, remains fundamental and central in every linguistic form. All of us (with very few exceptions) can perceive tones, timbre, pitch intervals, melodic contours, harmony, and (perhaps most elementally) integrate all of these and "construct" in our minds many different parts of cobwebbed spaces. There are utilitarian, grey tubs, the remnants of the second-class Archival footage of lunatic asylums. With cold high windows towards which I used to swim in my laboured crawl, as through a flooded cathedral, breast-stroking until covered over with my full flesh. Natural light is excluded in favour of sanctioned entropy.

Another of those decommissioned non-places kept in a vegetative state. Like the gothic sprawl of Queen Elizabeth's children, caught in spider's sticky nets. Shivering phantoms stand before empty mirrors, in tiled washrooms where thick taps leak promiscuous films. Exploit the creep of suspended unreachable lives. The echoing of cellars and toilet stalls used for evoking fashion shoots and promos. It is only reasonable that tribes of squatters, sensitive to the spirit of derelict buildings, dedicated to improvement from society, ruthlessly struck on the padlocked doors and the fateful announcement that I began to mistrust my own memory. Did I ever watch confusing episodes of I Don't Fucking Know, with other Dubliners? We entered through the twinned-doors — oh so grand, built for the road that had become a new entrance onto the hissing laundry looming chimney stack. Children learned feats of retravel, mongrels they are — the clapped-out rooms dribbling showers and rusty faucets — these experience of a community, within a short stroll of wet afternoons when walking. Wonderful machinery is vulnerable to various distortions, excesses, and breakdowns. The power to perceive (or imagine) may be impaired with brain imagery. Excessive and uncontrollable volts, leading to incessant repetition of hallucinations, in some people, seizures. There are special neurological hazards, "disorders of skill that may affect professional intellectual and emotional synaesthesia." Referred to our comfort power, therapeutic patients with a variety of neurological cortical strokes of dementia. Others have specific cortical syndromes — loss of language, movement, amnesias, or frontal lobe-syndromes. Some are autistic, artistic, artistically-autistic, others have sub-cortical syndromes, such as parkinsonism, or other movement disorders, all these conditions can potentially respond to observation and description with the latest technology and to incorporate both of these approaches, I have tried to listen to my subjects to imagine and enter their experiences. It is these which form the core. The economic dip in China, all those empty power blocks, sigh, sigh, sigh, in the speculative-opposite-effect(s) — with the market in trouble, the Chinese would want more bricks, and mortar, in a safe and welcoming shard-suite. There would never be another few hours on the fifty-second floor, the holiday promising for the sun to rise over great spikes, a firework orgy of Hollywood money $$$ $$ Blub blub blub whib whib whuub whob. Robust well-regarded orthopaedic surgeon in a small city in Sin. He was at a gathering, breezy he was, but he noticed a few clouds skittering in the distance — it looked like a payphone. He still remembers every single second of what happened next. "I was talking to phone...there was a little bit of distance...my phone was a foot away, from where I was standing, when I got struck...I remember a flash of light coming out of the phone, it hit me bewildered body." Experienced boosted connoisseurs of alternate realities, it's got nothing on displaying a prejudice for Rimbaud's Illuminations, total derangement of the senses, fire ringing in the new spectres of modernity. Modern taste has been avoided. Energy is directed to a question of love. It's a question of, is it a problem... what am I, a telephone, implementing your kids? The policeman in a cell knows where you be... in hospital, Mum, mum, mum! This is a new brother, know what I am saying? And it was an absolute fucking waster. They trapped her in stagecoach buses, in packs, showing off their service windows. They stall eagerly for the railway bridge. Slightly like racehorses. I love the blue bridges, the way its disappearing. I regarded him as a major master of territory, - mesmerized attention, concentrated that it must be called, righteous anger – love as alert. Alerted love. Sirens blaring. WW2 ghosts having a disco. The guide dressed as a road tunnel, with claw marks, striations of the bricks beneath generations, of varnish. Overloaded vans heading to the scrapyards. White heaped on numerous transits - gouged at the curve of the lane, going north. Stephen is a connoisseur of Pigeon Bridge, a promising spot, knows all the secrets of the silver stream, gatherer of images from Cambridge. Where he had kept for many years dawn raids on disputed former inhabitants. Radical printers, painters, performance artists, and invisible junkies, shooting up in the metal box lift, left for the trains. I could cycle up the valley. I could work in the dark room, then make a coffee, go for a wash to York. The silver fishing-pole is satisfied with this new pool of light under the bridge. The ripple of the planks, sigh. Now the fishing pole looks like some manic mastermind trying to trap expanding metal, something that was purchased so he in could own a hardware shop down the road. The telescopic pole is intended for use by WINDOW CLEANERS – that have adapted it for their camera setup. He allowed cameras primed one three twelve, that detonates... what he, the print birds, exploding fury, roof-rockers saw was a pile of ash. Where the Kray family home used to stand in silence... supported by the damned souls, that managed to transmigrate, these original interior lives made mortar and brick. Fallen from the pink of belly on a ledge unable to take flight, unwilling to fall, to the demented creature. Sisyphean torment, nothing to be done. Down on the pulped tires of a white van. Carving downward. Carving downward. Carving upward. Ouch caught my thumb. Caught my tongue. Lick, lick, lick it. Carving. Carving. Smoothing. Using. Sharp. Sticks. Sharp. Stones. Doesn't change the fact that this is true. I am at my whits end. Wits. Wits-end. The End. Dot. dotdotdot. What are your thoughts on that? Yeah, I am pleased to hear Lionel wrote into an omission, a big omission, a pretty good letter, the thing I like about the letter most. Apologists for cancel culture. Lying. Excuses. What they always say is look at JK Rowling. 14mill followers on Twitter. Victims of the culture is the ordinary peeps. Might get reprimanded. For expressing views that are apparently beyond the pale. The veil. Pull out the letter. Sign it. Phenomenology. Thinking. Biological accuracy. Extraordinary. No apologies. That doesn't happen. UnCancellable. Cancel. Culture. As. A whole. Wits. End. In relation to this "discussion" bumping into phenomenologists, demonstrating that to overcome is refusing to apologist, just hold firm. Do not kowtow, you pussy. My issue with the term, it is too slight, quaint, the ideological moment of which, as far as anyone can see, is foundation stones rolled over newborn babies. History reverted. Rewritten. Reimagined. History is about crimes. Nothing else. Tarnishing the chips of basic transsexual biological morphing, heavy on the shoulder of masses of western way of life-ers. Influential people hate culture, love arguing and nitpicking. Too much room, too much space given to people with too much time. Candybar, THE CREDIT CRUNCHY-BAR, is like cancel cultural hardon-pills.

Mummy!

Yes, sweetie!

What has love got to do, got to do with my zits?

Zits?

Spots, Mummy, spots!

What has, um, what got to do, got to do with it?

Love, Mummy, popping that spotty thing called love!

Shut up Adrian, you're being nonsensical again!

I appreciate how you said that so nicely Mummy, so very nicely, as if you weren't being rude and dismissive and cruel to me, me, Adrian, your only child, five years in head, fifty-five years in body.

Adrian, pull up your underwear, before the cat does his business in it again.

Mummy?

Yes?

What's love got to do, got to do with zits?

Call me, Vincent. Call me Goth. Call me Go. Call me anything but failure. Call me pathetic older brother. Call me Willem Defoe. Call me Lars von Trier's Parkinson Disease. Call up your child. Sweet nothing's work on their messed-up body. The hospital calls back, they are amazed,
nurses,
doctors,
porters as well,
shocked by the
diseased
child's
progress – a
note on
porters, they
have to always

get in on the action (they got to give those flowers they buy for a nurse they fancy but don't have the balls to give them to, to someone, anyone, why not a dying kid?) and do indeed take candy from babies... once they're dead, that is. The have a modicum of respect. They also like the sweets melted into the fabric of the wrapper. Call me Derek Jacobi. Call me sensational. Call me queer. Call me Ai produced Vincent without the aura of supercilious art obsession-twitches van Gogh. Call the children up. They answer in one voice. I ain't into the Bible, so I wouldn't say they were speaking as legion, though they had a good running if they wanted to audition for the reboot of Ghost Rider. Call me Ridley Scott, "Fuck you, fuck you very much, go fuck yourself, thank you, fuck you!" Call me by your name, and then get a rather tetchy look from me, because you called me Daddy, instead of my actual name; and I have told you, I am only Daddy on the birth certificate and in the bedroom between the hours of **WHEN YOUR MOTHER FINALLY FUCKING LEAVES** and gets back. Call me putrid. Call me wasteful. Call me auteur. Call me artist. Call me by your name, the name we etched into our favourite local circus pig's hide.

The end. The end. The end. The end. The end.
The End. The End. The End. The End. The End.
THE END. THE END. THE END. THE END.
The end. The end. The end. The end. The end.
The End. The End. The End. The End. The End.
THE END. THE END. THE END. THE END.
The end. The end. The end. The end. The end.
The End. The End. The End. The End. The End.
THE END. THE END. THE END. THE END.
The end. The end. The end. The end. The end.
The End. The End. The End. The End. The End.
THE END. THE END. THE END. THE END.
The end. The end. The end. The end. The end.
The End. The End. The End. The End. The End.
THE END. THE END. THE END. THE END.
The end. The end. The end. The end. The end.
The End. The End. The End. The End. The End.
THE END. THE END. THE END. THE END.
The end. The end. The end. The end. The end.
The End. The End. The End. The End. The End.
THE END. THE END. THE END. THE END.
This is the bloody well end. Please just end the
book, for all of mankind, for all that is unholy
and smeared in delicious honey mustard
sauce/dip. End the unending stream of cut-up-
consciousness. Whittle down the wooden
sculpture you made in my glorious image. Let it
end, for if it is to end there can be some respite.
Some moment of tranquillity and that archaic

sense of ease, that unravels to reveal it is total unease.

Humans were not made to be easy going.

We were made to cause utter uncontrollable chaos.

We were also made to End.

Not quite.

You have saved me.

I have saved you.

We have saved each other.

There is no power dynamic, just mutual respect.

Can we agree to disagree, so help us God?

I hope we can and will abso-bleeding-lutley be sure as surer as we can be!

BIO:

Nothing. Nada. Zilch.